JOURNEY FROM SURRENDER TO HOPE

RENU RAMACHANDRAN

I look into the mirror but do not see my reflection.

I see faces smiling back at me .

I look closely and recognise them

As people who have stood by me in my most difficult time.

I dedicate this book to all those who have given me
strength and continue to stand by me to this day.

Contents

Preface

This book is an account of my personal experience. I have shared my journey though an entire episode in my life. The incidents are real although details have been confined to the requirements of the book , to respect my privacy and also of the individuals involved.

I hope this resonates with the women , men and anybody who has been on a journey to find hope when it seems impossible.

Acknowledgements

I would like to thank my sister, Roopa, for proof reading the book and her suggestions; my daughter, Akshadha, for creating the book cover; my dear friend,Divya, for the beautiful book title; my daughter Anamitra for encouraging me. This book would not have been possible without your valuable contributions.

I would also like to thank Notion Press for publishing the book.

1

Geeta looked outside the window. She enjoyed the view from her room - open fields, the greenery, watching the cows and goats graze, the cow herds accompanied by their dogs keeping the herd in check, watching the flights taking off. The runway was close by. Watching the planes take off into the sky lifted her spirits as well. On rainy days, the planes soaring into the sky against the backdrop of black clouds was breath-taking. On days the wind direction changed, she would wake up to loud noises – engines revving up, it was deafening at times but so worth it.

Today as she sat looking outside the window, she saw neither planes, nor cows nor the greenery. It seemed that the world had quietened down, everything had come to a standstill. Was it her imagination? Her thoughts were interrupted by voices.

Mummy was calling. "Geeta, Geeta, where are the kids? Don't they have school today! They are always late to school. They haven't had breakfast. You should have woken them up earlier."

Geeta smiled – at least some things never change. She got up to see what the children were up to. As she was stepping out of the room, she looked at her reflection in the mirror. Her hair had turned grey – did she not colour it a week ago? Dark circles under her eyes - how long had it been since she had slept well? Are those age spots? – she couldn't remember having as many before. Her thoughts were interrupted yet again.

It was Mummy again – "Are they coming downstairs? What will they have for breakfast? Should I make something? Will you ask Zara not to lay on the staircase? Somebody is bound to fall one day. That's all we need – you falling."

"Coming Ma. Let me check on the kids", Geeta replied knowing that the barrage of questions will not stop until she responds.

Walking into the kids' room she noticed Rocky stretched on the bed, lying over the blankets fast asleep. Vibha was sitting up on the bed, earphones plugged into her ears. That was one sight Geeta couldn't stand first thing in the morning. "Vibha, Vibha ", she called. "Get off the phone this minute. Do you know what time it is? "

" Yes Mama, I am waiting for Vaishnavi to finish brushing her teeth" Vibha responded knowing that Mama did not like her being on the phone. At least now she was not in the line of fire.

Geeta walked to the bathroom door and knocked. "Vaishnavi, do you plan to spend the day there?" she asked.

"Almost done, Mama", came the reply from inside.

Geeta shook her head and walked out of the room signalling to Vibha to go down for breakfast. Rocky jumped off the bed sensing that Geeta was angry. He walked up to Geeta wagging his tail, threw himself on the ground, turned upside down waiting for Geeta to pet him. He looked so cute she couldn't resist kneeling on the floor beside him and rubbing his belly.

"Who is the naughty boy! who is the naughty boy, who is sleeping on the bed! Who is the little devil stretched on the blanket!", said Geeta playing with Rocky.

Hearing the change in Geeta's tone, Peaches, who was hidden under the bed came out and lay down next to Rocky to be petted. Jealous as he is, Rocky barked and snarled at Peaches as if to say "It's my time with Mama".

Geeta loved her dogs. They were her greatest stress busters. Although not trained to be emotional support animals, they did a great job calming her down. She walked back into her room. There was so much to do that day. She looked at the clock, it was half past 8. She would have to leave in an hour if she wished to visit the offices, she had planned to visit. She walked up to her closet where all the paperwork was kept, arranged in different folders and sorted just as Vidyuth had wanted it. He had always been meticulous when it came to documents.

He would always say, "Keep all important documents in a file, keep the files in a backpack. So, in case of a fire, you pick up the bag and run for your life."

So they always knew where the important documents were – bank papers, certificates, passports, property papers. Good practices, as Geeta always believed, should be followed. So that day when she had to look for documents, she had no trouble finding all that she needed. In the closet, inside the backpack,among the files – all arranged perfectly. She took out all the files, removed the required papers and documents and placed them in a separate file to carry. She checked on the girls once again to make sure they were getting ready for school and then went to get ready herself.

Breakfast was quick. She didn't want to waste time, else traffic would pick up and getting to the different offices would be a hassle. She had hired a driver for the day, there was a lot of driving to do, it could get exhausting. When she got to the door Mummy was ready with a bottle of water, a packet of biscuits and some advice-

"Ask the driver not to speed, it's alright if you have to make multiple trips. What will you do about lunch?".

"Ma, it's fine. I'll manage, and will stop at a place to eat when I am hungry", Geeta replied.

The girls came running down the stairs, hugged her, planted kisses on her cheeks, and Vaishnavi asked, "What will you get me?".

Children ! thought Geeta, every trip outside meant something had to be bought for them. "Let me see what stores are around there and then see what I can buy", She replied.

The dogs were quiet, they never liked people leaving. People visiting received a rousing welcome but when it was time to leave, they would refuse to say goodbye.

Geeta walked to the car, gave instructions to the driver and they left. It was a long journey; the closest office was an hour away. But by city standards an hour's drive was probably not as far at all. Geeta's mind was filled with thoughts. There was so much to do she just didn't want to think about it. She needed a distraction so she started a conversation with the driver.

"Where are you from?" she asked the driver in Hindi.

"I am a local here Madam, my ancestors moved into the city 3 generations ago. This is the only city I have known" he replied cheerfully.

"So, you must know the roads well. There must be a lot of traffic at this time in the city, isn't it?"

"Yes, Madam. You see, some years ago there was no problem getting from one place to another. But now it's very bad. "

The driver continued speaking about how routes had been converted to one-ways, where there were bottle necks, what roads to avoid at peak hours etc. Although Geeta wasn't following most of what was being said, she welcomed the distraction. At least her thoughts didn't bother her anymore. An hour went by and she reached the first office. Taking her file, purse and the bottle of water Geeta walked up the stairs to the office. These were the old buildings with no lifts. The steps were not dirty but they could have been cleaned better. Holding the railing was not a choice, no idea what had been wiped on them and she was sure they hadn't been cleaned in a long time.

Walking to the secondfloor she found the office. The guard outside pushed a register towards her and she entered the details. It was the usual – name, address, purpose, whom one is there to meet, time in and signature. She had always wondered why time out was never filled by the visitor. Maybe the guard was specifically told to ensure visitors made an entry before they entered the premises; they probably filled the time out when their shifts ended.

Shrugging these thoughts aside, Geeta entered the office. There were two people seated, the lady was already attending to a customer. The gentleman seemed free. He looked up at Geeta and offered her the seat before him. She sighed heavily, walked up to the chair, placed her purse on the side – clutching the file she said,

" My husband had 2 insurance policies with you. I have come to make a death claim for my husband. Can you please help?".

2

One Month Earlier

Shweta was in the room beside Vidyuth. Geeta was glad Shweta was there. It was quite overwhelming - the feeding, the changing, getting medicines, the multiple procedures. It was nice to watch Shweta playfully scolding her brother for being non -cooperative. Talking about incidents of when they were children and how Vidyuth had ratted her out to their parents. It really was a blessing not to be alone in a hospital and having to handle a critically ill patient especially in an unfamiliar city.

Vidyuth's condition had been critical since the time he was admitted. With each passing day it only worsened. While the doctors were very clear about the condition of his health and never gave any false hope, Geeta hoped he would recover. He had been on the ventilator for 4 days. Every time his condition worsened, Geeta would lose hope but she wouldn't admit it. How could she give up? He wasn't all that old. Besides, Vibha was waiting to celebrate her 12th birthday with him. He knew that. Geeta believed that he had no choice but to recover. She refused to believe his condition could get worse. He was in a hospital with the best doctors, he was being given medicines, everything to keep him going. That's what she had missed - the medicines were only keeping him alive. There was only that much medicines could do.

Geeta would have long conversations with Vidyuth while feeding and changing him. Although on the ventilator, she believed he could hear her. He may be staring into blank space, not responding, not blinking, but she believed in her heart that he could hear her. She would speak about the girls, about how naughty Rocky was becoming, share news snippets with him, play his favourite songs hoping something would trigger a response and he would get better. It was painful seeing him lying helpless, motionless, irresponsive, the multiple needle pricks, the number of IV lines connected to his body – but Geeta never cried in front of him. She believed if she lost hope, if she appeared weak, he would give up too. She would hold back her tears until she left the room.

The bathroom had become her refuge when she had a breakdown. She would excuse herself, lock herself in the toilet and cry her lungs out. There was not a day that went by when she did not cry. Crying had become a coping mechanism. It was like she had no control over the tear glands, they seemed to have a mind of their own. Something would trigger an alarm and the flood gates would open. If the bathroom was too far off then it was the back lane to the ward. Geeta could sit there and calm herself without being watched.

The doctors had nothing positive to share. The days there was no change, was a reason to celebrate – at least it hadn't taken a turn for the worse. Shweta was a pillar of strength; she ensured Geeta ate on time, took her vitamins, got her sleep. They took turns to watch over Vidyuth. Vidyuth's office also helped by sending people to cover the night.

Geeta loved to read. She had carried a book with her. She needed the distraction, anything to take her mind off the thousands of thoughts flooding her mind. There were relatives of other patients too. It was strange, Geeta thought, how people connected. All patients in the ward were critically ill, all faced the same challenges, all relatives were hopeful that their dear one would be discharged. That was what bonded the relatives. The struggle, the unknown outcome, the pain. It didn't matter where these people came from, what their backgrounds were, their faith, their interests, their beliefs – nothing mattered. They all shared their pain, their food, their time and most of all they were helpful to each other.

That day was no different from any other. Vidyuth's vitals had been stable. He had been fed. He needed to be changed but the ward boy was busy. A patient had been brought in and was declared dead by the doctor. There were a lot of formalities to be done before the body would be released to the next of kin. The ward boy was busy cleaning the body, preparing it to be transported by ambulance either to the mortuary or home. Geeta and Shweta waited for the ward boy to finish. It was quite late. They were yet to have dinner. They usually fed Vidyuth, cleaned him up and ensured the sheets were changed before they would retire to their room.

It was past 12:30 AM when the ward boy was finally free. Geeta went up to Vidyuth, but something seemed wrong. Vidyuth seemed to be gasping for breath. Geeta called the duty doctor and asked him to check Vidyuth. The doctor checked the monitor and realised the oxygen levels were dropping. Geeta had her eyes peeled to the monitor. The BP was beginning to drop too. Geeta moved away from the bed letting the doctor and nurses attend to Vidyuth. She continued staring at the monitor and then looked at Vidyuth. The BP and Oxygen were spiralling down – 65, 60, 55, ...45, 33... Geeta shifted her gaze from the monitor to Vidyuth and back. She ran up to the nurse and said,

" Do something! His oxygen and BP are plummeting"

The nurse looked at Geeta, tried to avert her gaze and said feebly," There is nothing we can do".

Geeta went back into the room and stared at Vidyuth. She urged him to fight it, "Come on Vidyuth! Come on! please!

Shweta walked into the room and coaxed Geeta to step outside. The room had all the doctors and nurses attending to Vidyuth. Geeta and Shweta waited outside the ward. They saw another doctor going into the room. After a while, one of the doctors walked up to them and asked Geeta,

"How are you related to him?"

Geeta replied," I am his wife."

"Your husband went into cardiac arrest. We tried our best. But we couldn't......" and his voice trailed off.

Geeta had to know for sure," He is no more?" she asked.

"Yes", said the doctor, averting her eyes.

"Ok. Ok", said Geeta. She walked away from the ward like in a trance and stood aside.

Shweta was standing right beside her. Sounding shocked, she said," What! Geeta! What is he saying, Geeta !"

Geeta barely heard anything that was being said to her. She was sobbing uncontrollably. Shweta held her and they both cried. After a while Shweta said

"Let's go see him, Geeta"

They went back into the room. There he was - lying on his bed. The tubes had been removed; the face had been wiped clean. His eyes were closed. He seemed so calm, so peaceful showing no signs of the struggle. Shweta and Geeta held each other and cried looking at Vidyuth. It seemed like they were still hoping that he would wake up. Time stood still. They had no idea how long they remained that way. Then Shweta left the room leaving Geeta alone with Vidyuth. Geeta still couldn't believe he was gone. She looked back at the monitor to see if there was any sign of him breathing. She walked up to him- passed her hand through his hair one last time, held his hand one last time. She squeezed his hand and said to him,

"Come back to me, Vidyuth. please come back to me. I love you."

She had no idea how long she stood there. She then wiped her tears, walked up to the doctor and told him, "I would like to take him back home."

It was past 1:45 AM. There was nothing that could have been done at that hour.

"He can be kept in the mortuary tonight until you make travel plans" suggested the doctor.

Geeta didn't know what to do. She called her sister, when Meghna answered the phone, Geeta blurted out, "He is gone, Meghna. He is gone." And she began to cry.

Shweta hugged her and held onto her. Meghna was crying too and woke up her husband. Geeta spoke to Jiju and said," I have to bring him back home, Jiju. Can you do something?"

"I am so sorry, Geeta. We will have to wait until tomorrow morning for anything to happen. If the hospital has a mortuary keep him there. We will fly him back tomorrow.", Jiju said.

Geeta just couldn't believe that nothing could be done in such emergencies. But she trusted her brother-in-law and knew that if there was something that could be done, he would certainly do it.

Geeta walked back to the doctor and told him that they would like to keep Vidyuth in the mortuary. The doctor handed Shweta a death certificate and arranged for an ambulance.

Vidyuth, by then, had been cleaned and wrapped up to be taken to the mortuary. They were helped into the ambulance and taken to the mortuary. There he was placed in C13.

Shweta ensured all was well before they were dropped back to their guest house. Both Shweta and Geeta were exhausted. It was 02:30 AM. They were completely drained of all energy. Geeta walked into the room as if in a dream. She walked into the bathroom, shut the door and cried. She couldn't believe it was all over. No more hope, no more prayers were required.

It was done. He was gone. She wouldn't see him again, would never feel his touch, would never see him smile, would never hear him complain. He was gone, gone forever.

When she had no more energy to cry, she walked back into the room, lay on the bed and closed her eyes. Exhaustion took over and she fell asleep.

3

Present Day

Sitting across from the Insurance claims officer, Geeta took out all the documents that would be required. The death certificate, Aadhar card – hers and Vidyuth's, their Pan cards, a cancelled cheque. The claims officer was helpful, he patiently took down all the information. Geeta sat there appearing very calm, but there was a storm brewing inside. She couldn't believe she was claiming insurance for Vidyuth. It felt so unreal, she imagined it was just a dream -a dream she would wake up from and all will be as before. Vidyuth will be packing for one of his travels, complaining about how badly his shirts had been ironed, how he couldn't find the matching pair of socks, giving her instructions on the bills that need to be paid, to ensure to keep the gate closed so the dogs wouldn't run out.

When the claims officer asked her the date of death, Geeta snapped out of her dream.

"10th Feb", she answered.

"Time of death?"

"12:55 AM ",

She was living it; it wasn't a dream. Her hands shook as she handed Vidyuth's Aadhar card and pan card. She couldn't see very well. Was it time to change her glasses? She hadn't checked her eyes in a while. But it wasn't the glasses, her eyes were moist. She couldn't cry, not now. This had to be done, no matter how hard it was, no matter how long it took, she needed to do this. Vidyuth was the sole earning member. She had bills to pay, she had a household to run.

"Hang on Geeta! Hang on !", she said to herself. There will be a time for grief but that time was not now. She had offices to visit, documents to submit, this took time and time was what she didn't have. She waited for all the process to complete, once she received the confirmation that the claim request had been successfully placed, she thanked the officer and left. As she climbed down the stairs, she felt faint. Did she not have breakfast? She couldn't remember what she had eaten. She reached out for the bottle of water that was in her bag. She gulped down some water, feeling better she climbed down the rest of the stairs and headed for the car.

Time to visit the next office. When she reached the building, she realised the lift wasn't working – there was a power cut and they had no power back up. The office was on the 5th floor. Geeta wondered that maybe this was not just a test of mental and emotional strength but also physical strength. She slowly walked up the stairs one floor at a time. She finally reached the 5th floor. She was breathless. She was about to push through the door, when the guard stopped her and asked her to make an entry in the register. Geeta couldn't help but smile. Power or no power, lift or no lift – there was no way to get past the register......

Having entered the details, she walked into the office and walked up to the reception.

"I am here to make a death claim", she said.

Thankfully, the lady who had advised them to take the policy, was there. She was very helpful. She took Geeta into a separate cabin and gave her the form to be filled, while she took copies of all the relevant documents.

Geeta filled the first blank. Name of the insured: Vidyuth …. She couldn't write anything else. She choked. She was glad she was alone in the cabin. She didn't want to cry in front of people. She swallowed hard, sipped some water and continued writing.

Next was the date of death, then came time of death. "How many more of these would she have to fill, how many times would she have to fill them?" What Geeta didn't know at that moment was that this was just the beginning. There would be so many places, so many more forms, so many more times of reliving the trauma in the days to come. She finished filling the forms, completed the formalities.

The lady was full of empathy. She had met Vidyuth. She was making small talk, expressing her shock at the turn of events. Geeta was smiling, listening, nodding, she didn't want to seem impolite. But she wanted to run, she wanted all of this to stop, she just wanted to run away from the lady, from the office, from reality. This could not be happening to her. The insurance money was for their old age, when the kids were grown up, for them to enjoy their retired life. Until that time, she had never asked the question "Why?". "Why was this happening to her?'. She had accepted this as her fate but then sitting in that cabin she couldn't understand why it had to be this way. Her fate, she could deal with, she had been through tough times before, but the children … This can't be their fate. They were still young. They had yet to reach adolescence. They were yet to have girl friends or boyfriends. Vidyuth had said," I better build some muscles before the girls start dating. There is no way any boy gets anywhere close to them". How Geeta would laugh!

"The claim has been made; you should receive the amount in 5 days' time" the lady was saying. I do know these are difficult times, but you should invest for your old age too. Later I will share plans to suit your requirements. Take care."

Geeta was still in a daze. She got up, thanked the lady and started walking out of the office. Did she hear her right ! Did the lady just offer her another insurance plan! Geeta knew she meant well but at that moment Geeta had no idea what she wanted. Her head was reeling. She walked down the stairs, got into the car and closed her eyes.

The chatty car driver was his usual chirpy self.

"Where do we go now, Madam?", he asked.

It was late and they hadn't had lunch. Geeta asked the driver to stop at an eatery. She got off and he drove away. She chose a table away from the crowd. Looking around brought back memories of when she and Vidyuth had dinner at the same eatery with friends a few years ago. It was so much fun – there was live music, cocktails and seafood. Vidyuth loved lobsters, crabs and prawns. He always enjoyed the starters. He was also the perfect host. Always stocked up on the snacks and drinks. Would make his own egg bhurji or honey chicken and fried rice. No matter how hard Geeta tried she could never make it the way he did.

Geeta ordered her meal and waited. Vidyuth was a good cook but he had to get into the mood to cook. How she missed those times – watching Vidyuth clear out the kitchen counter to cook a meal. He would ask Geeta to leave the kitchen, play his favourite songs and get started. He would neatly spread out a newspaper on the counter, place the cutting board, knife and peeler on it. He would choose the vegetables, wash them, pat them dry, cut and clean them. He would choose the biggest pan, the biggest cooking pot, and pour a generous amount of oil or butter. Fry the onions to perfection, add the vegetables or chicken, pour salt, chilli and masalas to it and would never use a measuring spoon. Geeta never knew how he managed to get the spices right every time. She would joke about it and say he probably ran a fast-food joint in his last birth.

Geeta quietly ate her meal and planned the rest of the evening. She would have to leave before the girls got home after playing. She had to pick up something for them. She ordered pizza, momos and pasta to carry back home. The girls would like that. She left with the parcel, got into the car and they drove towards home. She made a few purchases on the way and of course got a tour guide version of the city from the driver. She didn't mind it at all. It was a welcome distraction. She was tired, she eased into the seat, rested her head on the back rest and listened to the pleasant chatter of the driver.

The drive back took longer, traffic had picked up. Geeta heard her phone ring. It was Vibha

"Where are you, Mama?"

"On my way, darling."

"How much longer?"

"Hmmm. Another half an hour!"

"So long! But you were gone all day."

"I know. It takes time travelling from one place to another. Then it takes time at each office."

"Did you have lunch, Mama?"

"Yes, darling. I also bought some stuff for you two."

"Vaishnavi! Mama has bought us dinner."

Geeta smiled. She could hear Vaishnavi sounding all excited.

"Really! Wow!

"Let me get home, you both do some reading. Did the dog walker take the doggos out?"

"Yes, Mama. He brought them back soon though and he didn't brush them." That was typical of Vibha, the dogs meant everything to her. If she had to choose between saving a human or a dog – the choice would be easy – she would save the dog.

"Ok. I will speak to him tomorrow."

After battling traffic, Geeta got home. The dogs gave her a rousing welcome. Vibha hugged her, Vaishnavi took the food packet from her saying,

"Oooo! What did you buy, Mama?"

Mummy was anxious too.

"What took you so long? I was about to call you when Vibha said she had spoken to you. Do you want some tea?"

"Yes Ma. ``Saying this Geeta walked up to her room, dumped the folder and purse on the bed, walked into the bathroom, turned on the tap, shut the door, buried her face in the towel and cried out loud.

"Come back Vidyuth! please come back!

4

One Month Earlier

"Wake up Geeta !" Shweta was calling her .

Geeta was groggy. She had slept as if drugged. What time of the day was it! Shweta must be leaving for the hospital, she thought. That's when it struck her, no more hospital, Vidyuth was ready to go home. She sat up on the bed. Shweta was saying something.

"Geeta! Geeta! You want me to get coffee for you?"

"Yes. Thanks Shweta. You can take the room keys; I will freshen up by then."

"Jayanth is coming. He will get here in an hour's time." Jayanth was Vidyuth's cousin.

"Ok. That's good. Will help with all the running around."

Geeta could not imagine doing all of it by herself. Clear the hospital bills, get the coffin made, the process of embalming, getting the necessary certificates. Her head was reeling.

Shweta left to get coffee. Geeta got up, walked into the bathroom. She began brushing her teeth. She looked at herself in the mirror, tears began rolling down her cheeks. She leaned towards the mirror and began sobbing. She then washed her face, blew her nose, reached for the towel and cried into the towel. Finally, when no tears would come, she had a shower, changed and got ready to make arrangements to take Vidyuth home. Shweta walked in just then and gave her coffee. The coffee was good, the best the hospital canteen had to offer. Also, thanks to Shweta, in 2 weeks the canteen boy knew exactly how she liked her coffee.

It felt good, sipping the warm coffee. Just then the phone rang, it was Vidyuth's boss. They were booking tickets and making arrangements for Vidyuth's final journey back home. This was to be his last flight ever. For someone who had constantly been travelling, practically lived out of a suitcase most of his life, this would be the last time he would take a flight. Geeta fought back tears, sharing passenger details. In the meanwhile, Jiju was arranging to have the coffin taken to the mortuary once they landed, the arrangements for cremation the next day and arranging logistics once they landed.

It was decided that they would take the last flight so that all other formalities would be completed by then. Jayanth had reached. Geeta had stepped out to have breakfast. When she got to the room, Jayanth opened the door. He waited for Geeta to walk into the room, he hugged her and said,

"I am so sorry, Geeta didi".

Geeta broke down. Jayanth held her until she calmed down. The people from Vidyuth's office were already at the hospital, talking to authorities and sorting out the paperwork. Jayanth went with them to help. Shweta stepped out too, as the hospital needed some clarifications. Geeta sat alone in the room. Vidyuth's office staff had brought his belongings all packed in his suitcase and some things stuffed in a bag. Vidyuth never liked carrying polythene bags. Geeta spread the things from the bag on the bed. She opened up one of Vidyuth's suitcases, moved things around to make space for other stuff. She opened her suitcase too and began rearranging it. As she was packing, tears streamed down her cheeks - there were his shirts, his perfume, his files. She continued rearranging the suitcases as if in a trance. It was all finally done. Just the way Vidyuth would have liked it.

Senior staff from Vidyuth's office had come to pass on their condolences. Geeta maintained her composure. She thanked them for the assistance and support they provided during the hospital stay and got ready to leave for the airport. She kept Meghna updated on all that was happening. Meghna had already informed the girls about Vidyuth, Geeta couldn't imagine what they must be going through. They were just so young. She wanted to be with them, hold them, reassure them that she was still with them. That Vidyuth would be with them in spirit, he would watch over them.

The staff at the airport was cordial too. Geeta waited at the cargo section. Vidyuth would be brought in the coffin to the cargo section. She didn't want there to be delays because of paperwork. She filled all the details, forms, provided the documents and waited. Jayanth reached with the coffin. All the papers were verified – the coffin maker's certificate, the embalming certificate. Once everything was done, Geeta walked towards the terminal. As she reached the entrance, she turned around, thanked Vidyuth's staff and walked into the airport teary eyed.

The flight was slightly delayed. Geeta was getting restless. All she wanted was to get home. Finally, the flight arrived and they boarded. After meals were served on the flight, exhaustion took over and Geeta fell asleep. She woke up as the plane touched down. It was past midnight. They got off the flight, collected their bags and walked out of the terminal building. Geeta saw Meghna waiting for her. Geeta walked up to her and hugged her. They held each other for a while and cried. It felt good to be back home, be back with family. They drove to the cargo section, collected Vidyuth's remains. He was driven to the mortuary in an ambulance, Jayanth accompanied the ambulance. Jiju drove them home. It all felt so unreal. Vidyuth was all about drama. His life had always been exciting. Frequent travels, he never liked staying in one city for too long. Geeta didn't know if that was the end he would have wanted but it sure was a dramatic one.

They drove in silence. Geeta asked Meghna,

"How are the girls?"

"They are ok. They cried a bit but seemed composed. I really don't know, Geeta. I tried really hard not to break down while talking to them. I had tears in my eyes as I spoke to them, we all cried a little. "

"How's Ma?", Geeta asked.

"Inconsolable ", replied Meghna.

Geeta sighed. It was worse for the mothers. They plan and dream about their child's future, pray for their well-being, their prosperity. What they never expect is such a sudden turn of events and losing someone younger while they are still alive. She didn't want to think about what it must be like for Vidyuth's mother. Couldn't imagine facing any of them. She felt like she had failed them all. She had left convinced that he would recover and they would return together. But here she was coming back with only his mortal remains. As they approached home, she kept telling herself,

"Get a hold of yourself, Geeta! Don't cry. Not now. Not now. "

Everybody got out of the car one after the other. The dogs rushed to the door. – Crying, wailing, jumping. Seeing them made her forget all the pain, all the grief. She petted them for a while. Walked up to Ma, hugged her. Walked to Vidyuth's mother, hugged her. The girls were upstairs. Dad was asleep, so Geeta walked upstairs to the girls. Meghna and Shweta were talking to the mothers. Geeta knew she couldn't deal with it now. She had to see the girls. She had to know how they were doing. They were awake waiting for her. They ran up to her and hugged her. Geeta felt a sense of relief as she held them. She was holding onto them rather than the other way round. She knew that moment that if there was anything that would pull her through this, it was them. She needed them more than they needed her.

"Did you have dinner, Mama?", Vibha asked Geeta.

"I ate poha on the plane, darling. You haven't slept yet?"

"We were waiting for you, "said Vaishnavi.

"You should sleep now. We have to give dada a final farewell tomorrow."

"Where is dada?", asked Vaishnavi.

"He is at the mortuary."

"Why, Mama? Why can't he be here?"

"He was unwell, so they have wrapped him up and will keep him safe there. We will see him tomorrow. Ok! Now get some sleep. Mama hasn't slept either and I am tired."

"Good night, Mama", said Vibha.

"Good night, Mama", said Vaishnavi.

"Good night, darlings ", said Geeta smiling at them. They are angels, she thought.

Geeta could hear Shweta and Meghna leave. She walked into her room, showered, changed and got ready to sleep. She had 2 companions for the night- Rocky and Peaches. They had already staked claim to their respective places on the bed. Geeta couldn't help but smile. She hugged them, kissed them on the forehead and lay down. It was cold, had been raining for a few days. She got up and took out Vidyuth's bathrobe from the wardrobe. She wrapped it around herself and lay down.

Geeta shut her eyes, the scene from the hospital played back in her mind - Vidyuth struggling, the oxygen levels dropping, the BP plummeting. She couldn't sleep. She stared out of the window. The wind direction had changed. She could hear the planes revving up their engines ready for take-off. Vidyuth would never fly again. She would never run through the packing check list with him again. There would never be long instructions and to do lists. No more goodbyes. This was it. She would bid him farewell once last time.

Geeta looked at the ring on her finger. She adjusted it. It was the ring Vidyuth gave her when he proposed to her. He had gone down on one knee. Geeta had been so embarrassed, the ring had been loose. But she wore it all the same, every day until they got married, before it got replaced by the wedding ring.

It was all coming to an end. He was walking out of her life just like he had walked in all those years ago. It was just too soon, way too soon. Could things not have been different? She wasn't ready to let him go.... No .... Not yet. She buried her head in the bath robe and began sobbing.

Come back Vidyuth! please come back!

5

Present Day

It was Vibha's birthday in a few days. In spite of all that happened, Geeta wanted to celebrate Vibha's birthday. Vidyuth had made plans for the day too. He was to take time out from work, invite the entire family to the birthday and as he would say -- "Relax!" He had planned to drive down to bring mom in law home, and have the entire family together. An occasion to celebrate. He had it all planned.

"We will put the dogs inside the house. Let's decorate the garage and cut the cake there. We can place the chairs on the side for the kids. We can have the family over for dinner, get the cook to make Biryani and he can make some sweet too – How about Gajar ka Halwa? And ask him not to put whole cardamom in it. All these cooks think adding extra spice enhances the taste. "

Geeta never understood what it was with Vidyuth and cooks. He would have complaints about all that they cook – "it's too salty! it's too spicy! Why are there pieces of ginger in this? "

In fact, he had once asked if the fried rice the cook made was better than what he made. Geeta had laughed so hard that tears rolled down her cheeks.

"Are you in competition with the cook !", she had asked.

"No, just checking if he meets my standards", was his reply.

Nobody could make fried rice the way Vidyuth did. She could still taste the fried rice he would make.

"Mama, Vaishnavi has locked the bedroom door again! She is late and she'll get everybody else late."

Geeta was brought back to the present with Vibha's complaint. They were to go shopping for birthday supplies - Balloons, decorations, return gifts etc.

Geeta walked to the girl's bedroom and knocked on the door.

"Vaishnavi, open the door! Let Vibha get her clothes out.
"

"I am almost done, Mama."

"She is lying, Mama. She just locked the door. She'll take an hour inside. I know it. She always does this"

"Vibha! Stop it! She will open the door in 5 mins. If she doesn't, I will get her to open the door. Why don't you go downstairs and take some shopping bags and fill a bottle of water? Come on! Let's not fight."

"She always does this. She knew I was going to take my clothes. She is so annoying !"

"Come on, Vibha! She isn't all that bad."

"She is Mama. And she is worse."

Vibha walked down the stairs frowning.

Geeta walked up to the girl's room and knocked on the door.

"Vaishnavi! 5 mins? Ok Darling."

"Ok Mama! I am combing my hair"

Geeta shook her head. Girls! They could find a million reasons to pick up a fight.

She walked back to her room. She chose her clothes, got dressed. But she couldn't find her socks. She preferred shoes when there was a lot of walking to do. And shopping with the girls would involve a lot of walking. She looked through all the shelves, no sign of socks. It was high time she had set her wardrobe right. She could never find her things. She looked towards Vidyuth's wardrobe. There were socks there. She stood staring at the wardrobe, sighed loudly and opened it. She pushed through his suits, moved the shirts. She had a strange feeling in her stomach. She then moved his jeans – he usually put the socks in a corner next to the jeans. Her heart was pounding. Her eyes fell on the shirt Vidyuth had worn the day he was admitted to the hospital. It was tucked away in the corner. She must have kept it there the day she emptied his suitcase. Without any warning, tears rolled down her cheeks. She held onto the shelf; her head was spinning ....

"Mama! Vibha is using my comb! she has dandruff in her hair, I'll get it now."

Geeta composed herself and wiped her tears.

"Vaishnavi! Her dandruff is all gone. Don't worry. And Vibha! Where is your comb? Do you have to fight about everything?"

Geeta continued looking for the socks. She found it behind the jeans. She took it out and shut the wardrobe. Her heart was still pounding. She walked downstairs, warmed some tea, sat down at the dining table and slowly sipped the tea.

Meghna had said she would drive them to the mall. Rocky began barking and whining.

"He barks at everything and everybody as if he owns the place." Mummy was saying.

"It's Meghna Ma! He is greeting her. "

Meghna had just reached the door – Zara, Peaches and Rocky ran up to her to greet her.

"I am getting mauled here, "cried Meghna. "I have only 2 hands, you have to wait your turn ", she was telling the dogs.

The girls came down all ready to go. Akanksha, Meghna's daughter was there too. She was home after her exams. They drove to the mall. Akanksha and the girls got busy shopping for birthday stuff. Meghna and Geeta were looking for all that they needed for the snacks and lunch. Meghna was very organised; she had made a list of all that was needed. Geeta relied on her for all that needed perfection.

The best part about super markets were the range of products, the worst part - the long wait for billing. After finally paying up, loading the car with bags, they were all ready to leave when

"Mama, can we get the cone ice cream?" That was Vaishnavi, the one with the sweet tooth.

Geeta and Meghna looked at each other and rolled their eyes.

"Please, Mama! It has been so long since I had ice cream, I mean cone Ice cream".

Akanksha volunteered to take them.

"I'll take them Geeta aunty".

With everybody finally getting what they wanted, they drove back.

Having put the groceries away and having had lunch, Geeta was resting. The girls were busy making invites for the birthday. A message popped up on Geeta's phone. The insurance claim had been processed; the money would be credited in 2 days. She looked out of the window, one by one everything linked to Vidyuth's existence was getting wiped out. Very soon all that would be left would be his belongings that she would hold onto, photographs and of course the scores and scores of memories that they had built over the years.

Vibha walked into the room interrupting Geeta's thoughts. She lay down next to Geeta and hugged her. Geeta kissed her on her forehead and held her close.

And of course, thought Geeta, the most precious gift that Vidyuth had left behind were the girls, so she could carry on living.

6

One Month Earlier

Geeta woke up to the sound of barking. Rocky was barking his head off at somebody. It was one of the guards on his morning rounds. She looked at the time, it was past 6 AM. Time to get up. She could hear mom in law waking up the girls. She had come to live with Geeta when Vidyuth had been hospitalised. Being alone in her own house she had been getting anxious and restless. She was sharing the room with the girls. It was a blessing having everybody around at a time like this.

Geeta woke up slowly. Today was the day. Rocky ran and jumped onto the bed. He lay down and raised his paw. Geeta rubbed his belly, kissed him and lay down hugging him. Mom in law walked to the room and said,

"Geeta! The kids are getting ready. Shweta said they will be here by 9:00. I am going down to help with breakfast."

"Ok. Mummy", replied Geeta.

Shweta and family were staying at Meghna's place. Geeta walked into the girl's room. Vibha was in the bathroom. Vaishnavi walked up to her and said,

"Mama! Today is your wedding anniversary, isn't it? Don't worry! We will celebrate it in a grand way."

Geeta broke down; it was a cruel twist of fate. She couldn't contain her tears. She hugged Vaishnavi and they both cried. Wiping her tears and then Vaishnavi's, Geeta said

"Thank you, my darling. Don't cry. We have to get ready and say goodbye to dada."

"What will we do, Mama?"

"Remember how when badi Dadi had died we piled wooden logs, placed Dadi on it and lit it on fire? We will do the same today."

"Then Dada will go to heaven?"

"Yes, he will. We do it properly, he will be happy. We all have to be there to say goodbye to him. So, get dressed quickly and let's be ready before Meghna aunty comes."

Geeta walked back to her room, shut the door and cried. She had hoped Vidyuth would get better before their anniversary. She had even whispered in his ear while in the hospital that they would celebrate their anniversary together, even if it were in the hospital. It hadn't occurred to her that the girls would remember the date.

She got dressed, walked down and had breakfast. The girls were already downstairs and were having breakfast. Neither of the mothers had eaten. Geeta looked at them – faces swollen, red-eyed, tears welled up in their eyes. Geeta could only imagine what it must be like for them. One having lost a young son, the other seeing her daughter widowed. She tried to get them to eat. They managed to take a bite.

Meghna reached. Jiju was driving. They all got into the car. Shweta also had their car. Everybody got in. They all drove in silence to the cemetery. Vidyuth had already been brought in and was laid on the pyre. Geeta could see people at the cemetery, just didn't know who. It all felt like a dream. She told herself she could do this. She had to be brave for the mothers, for the girls. She started walking up to the pyre, head down, trying to hold back tears. There were tombstones on either side of the path leading up to the pyre. She tried not to look at them. Half way through the path Geeta's resolve broke. She stopped, turned away, covered her eyes with her hands and cried. She couldn't do this... she wasn't ready to say goodbye.

She felt hands on her shoulder, comforting her. Geeta stopped crying, wiped her tears, pulled herself together and continued walking up the path. She met relatives, she enquired how they had come and when they arrived. She walked up to Vidyuth's friends enquiring about when they got there and if they were staying. She continued walking to the pyre, she had to see Vidyuth. Somebody stopped her and hugged her. Geeta hugged back. It was a dear friend, Lata. She heard Jiju speaking to Vidyuth's uncles about the rites that needed to be performed.

Geeta turned back and saw Vidyuth's ex-wife Deepthi and son, Krish walk up to her. She was glad they had come. Krish hugged her and they both cried. He was a lot taller than her now. Vidyuth's cousins walked up to them and asked Krish to accompany them. He was performing the last rites. He had to change into a dhoti. Vidyuth's ex-wife, Deepthi, walked up to Geeta and hugged her.

One by one everybody walked up to the pyre to pay their last respects to Vidyuth. Geeta took the girls to Vidyuth, Krish walked up to the pyre, walked away to a corner and started crying. Somebody from the family was consoling him. Meghna brought Mummy and Shweta brought Mom in law to Vidyuth. They could barely walk. We were then asked to move away. Geeta took one last look at Vidyuth and walked to a corner. She could barely see where she was going. She was crying inconsolably. Krish was being guided by the cemetery staff on what needed to be done.

Geeta stood at the corner watching. Lata stood next to her with her arms around Geeta. Geeta continued crying constantly saying," Come back Vidyuth! Come back ! in the back of her mind. The pyre was lit. He was gone. First the mind, now the body. There will be nothing left of him. Geeta was lost in her grief. She had her eyes fixed at the pyre. She watched the pyre burn until the cemetery staff asked them to move away.

Geeta walked away and saw Shweta. She broke down again and said to Shweta

"He is gone Shweta, he just decided to end everything and he left."

Shweta hugged Geeta and tried to console her. Geeta then looked for the girls. Vaishnavi was crying loudly. "Dada is gone, Mama! Dada is gone. He will never come back Mama. I will never see him again."

Geeta did not know what to tell her anymore. She just held her and they both cried. Geeta couldn't find Vibha. She asked Shweta if she had seen Vibha. She saw Vibha with Meghna. Vibha was holding back her tears; she had a purse in her hand that she clutched so tight that her fingers had turned white. She looked blankly at Geeta fighting back her tears. But she wouldn't cry. Geeta pulled Vibha towards her and hugged her. Still no tears. Vibha was being brave for Geeta. Geeta then looked for Krish. He was standing at the far end and was being consoled by Geeta's cousin. The mothers were already in the car.

Geeta spoke to Vidyuth's friends who were leaving. She said her goodbyes to all those who had come. She walked to the car and climbed in exhausted. As they drove back, Vaishnavi began crying again,

"I'll never see Dada again, Mama. We'll never have dinner together; we won't go out together. He wont be here for our birthdays, Mama!"

Geeta tried consoling her but she wouldn't stop crying. All Geeta could do was hold her and let her cry it out. Vibha sat silently clutching the bag tight, looking at Vaishnavi. She then looked at Geeta, who smiled at her. Vibha looked back at Vaishnavi and then looked out of the window.

Vaishnavi continued crying. Geeta held her until she stopped. At least she was letting it all out. Geeta was worried about Vibha. There was no way of knowing what she was thinking. Geeta was amazed at how Vibha was holding up for her. She knew Vibha was being strong for her, lending her support. If only Vidyuth could have seen her that moment, he had always been proud of the way Vibha was growing up to be a sensible, loving, caring girl.

Geeta leaned back on the seat, rested her head against the back of the seat and looked out the window. She was tired. A wave of fatigue swept through her. She was staring out the window but this time there were no thoughts. The rest of the trip back home was quiet. All lost in their own thoughts, feelings and grief. Geeta had no energy left to console anybody.

When they got home, everybody had to shower. The girls went up with Mom in law. Mummy went into her room. Deepthi and Krish went to Geeta's room to shower. Geeta waited for them to finish. It was almost lunch time. Jiju came with food. Everybody went down for lunch. Geeta needed some alone time. So much had taken place in 40 hrs, she was still coming to terms with what had happened.

"Geeta! Come down for lunch! "It was Meghna.

"Will shower and come. Ten mins!" Geeta replied.

Geeta took her change of clothes, walked into the bathroom, shut the door. She turned the tap on to fill the bucket. She sat on the stool and stared at the walls. Water began overflowing. A knock on the door shook Geeta.

"Geeta! You done!" It was Meghna again.

"Yes! Almost. I'm coming"

There were no tears this time. Her eyes had dried and they were hurting, her head hurt, her chest hurt. She managed to shower. The warm water felt good. It was soothing. She wasn't hungry, just tired. She wished she could sleep. She dragged herself downstairs, ate some food and went back up to sleep.

She lay down. The last rites had to be performed. They were speaking about it in the hall. Geeta could hear the discussion. Vidyuth's uncles had asked her how she wanted it done. Geeta was adamant, it had to be the 3rd day. Vidyuth would have never wanted a long-drawn ritual. Besides, the girls were already going through so much, she couldn't let anything affect them anymore.

Had the girls informed the school about their leave of absence? Meghna must have done that, thought Vibha. Geeta was tired but she couldn't sleep.

"If only I could get some sleep", thought Geeta, "I'll feel so much better". `` I wonder if the girls have been up to date with their homework. Vaishnavi must be lagging behind in her assignments.... I should talk to their teachers and ask for time....... "

Fatigue finally took over and Geeta fell asleep.

Present Day

The room was a mess. Toys all over the floor, clothes strewn on the bed and the chairs, papers and books all over the study table. Geeta couldn't imagine how the girls managed to live in the room. She decided to clean it up but didn't know where to start. She first picked the clothes, sorted and folded them. Stacked up the books and the papers, she wasn't doing the toys. She called out to them.

"Girls! Put away your toys! Vibha, Vaishnavi, put away your clothes, keep the books in the drawers. God! Is that paint on the bed? Why can't you put things away after you use them? "

That tone, the girls, knew meant trouble. They stopped doing whatever it was they were doing. Vibha started putting the toys away. Vaishnavi was putting away her clothes. Geeta wanted to sort out her cupboards as well. But she needed the girls to finish first and go out to play.

"Mama! I put my clothes in my cupboard and put the toys away", said Vibha.

"I have finished too, Mama!"

That was quick, thought Geeta. She walked into their room and it seemed reasonably clean.

"Can we go out to play, please?", asked Vaishnavi.

"Ok! But come back for lunch."

"Ok Mama!"

"Don't make me come and call you"

"Ok Mama"

"And do not go inside anybody's house. Play in the park."

"Ok Mama!"

They gave her a kiss and went out to play. Geeta looked at the time. She had 2 and a half hours before they came home for lunch. She had been planning to do this for a while but she couldn't get herself to do it. Today is the day, she thought. Walking back to her room she opened Vidyuth's wardrobe. She had told Krish she would send Vidyuth's clothes to him. They'd fit him perfectly . That's what Vidyuth would have wanted as well.

She looked at the suits all dry cleaned and yet to be worn. The formal shirts were all ironed and neatly stacked. She brought out a cardboard box, lined it up with cling wrap and dropped some naphthalene balls in them. She removed the formal shirts from the cupboard and stacked them up one over the other in the box. Some of these shirts were her favourites too, the one he wore the first time they met, she picked up a shirt and felt it against her cheek. She passed her hand over the other shirts; she will never see him wear them again. Tears rolled down her cheeks. She had to keep the shirts away so that her tears didn't fall on them. She opened the suitcases that had his clothes. She hadn't opened them until then.

Once she was done with the shirts, she moved to the trousers, then the suits. After a while she could barely see what she was packing. She was sobbing. It seemed like she had no control over her tears any more. But she had to admit that crying helped her cope. When she kept her feelings bottled in, she would feel an ache in her chest, her abdomen, she would feel faint and nauseous. But when she cried, she felt lighter and the ache and uneasiness seemed to disappear. At the moment it felt good just to let the tears flow.

Once the suits were done, she packed all his ties and shoes. She then reached the stack of t-shirts. She couldn't pack those; she had seen him wear them around in the house. She couldn't give them away. She leaned into the wardrobe, lay her head on the clothes and cried. The clothes smelt of him. She wasn't ready to part with all of his belongings as yet. She decided to keep the t-shirts.

Two boxes had been filled. Geeta wrapped up the clothes and closed the boxes. She felt drained of all energy. She slumped into the recliner and looked at the boxes, she realised she hadn't packed the cuff links. She got up, opened the draw, took out the bag with the cuff links and placed them in the box. She wondered if she should pack his perfumes. She decided against it. She then taped the boxes and labelled them. She walked back to the room, wrapped herself in Vidyuth's bathrobe and closed her eyes. Tears were still streaming down her face. She wiped the tears, clutched the bath robe tight and fell asleep.

Geeta had no idea how long she slept. She heard Vibha kissing her on her cheek and waking her up. "Mama! Nani wants to know if you will have lunch."

Geeta had no energy to walk down stairs nor was she in any state of mind to strike a conversation with her mother. She told Vibha,

"Can you please get some rice, dal and sabzi for me, darling. Please?"

"Ok Mama". Saying this Vibha went downstairs and served a plate for Geeta. Geeta could hear her mother asking Vibha "Is Mama not coming downstairs?"

"No Nani. She is tired and sleepy. I will take the plate upstairs to her"

God bless Vibha ! thought Geeta. There had been so many occasions that Vibha had come to her rescue. At times, it seemed like she was the most mature member of the family.

Geeta had lunch and watched some tv to divert her mind. She could hear the girls playing with their Lego sets. She could hear Vibha laugh, Vaishnavi was a very good story teller and was very witty. They were darlings! Geeta wondered what she would have done without them. They were the reason she could go on.

Geeta hadn't been downstairs all morning, so she decided to have the evening tea with her father. Dad was already enjoying his cup of tea when Geeta walked downstairs.

"Enjoying your tea, Dad !"

"Yes. Nothing like a good cup of tea. "He seemed to be in a good mood.

"I had a good time today," Dad was saying.

"That's nice", Geeta said.

"I met Bhaskar Mama today. It felt good seeing him after all these years. I am glad I made the trip. "

"That's nice , Dad. How is he? "asked Geeta.

"He is well. His business is doing very well."

"That's nice. He must have been happy to see you."

"Oh yes! We had lunch together, and I met his staff. It was good."

Geeta looked at her dad, he was smiling. It had been a while since she had seen him so relaxed and happy.

She didn't tell him that Bhaskar Mama had passed away 13 years ago. She didn't remind him of the past or correct him. There was no point because he would forget again. Dementia had started taking its toll on him. He hadn't even noticed that Vidyuth was not around. It was a blessing in disguise, Geeta thought, he didn't have to deal with the pain of losing a dear one. She wished there was some way she could forget all of this too. Erase all the painful memories.

An alarm rang on the phone. It was a reminder to pay the house rent. Geeta sighed! There was pain, grief, sadness but there were also bills that needed to be paid. She knew they couldn't go on like this forever. It was time she started looking for work. It had been a long break from her career. Will she find work? Will she be hired? Will she fit in? One thing at a time, she said to herself, One thing at a time. She would enjoy tea with dad today. She will think about applying for jobs tomorrow.

Tomorrow is another day! Tomorrow is another day!

8

One Month Earlier

Geeta woke up wondering what the time was. She did not hear the alarm ring so she assumed that it was earlier than 6 AM. She continued to lay down, stroking Peaches who was lying next to her. The mothers were up and about. She could smell the tea being made. She wished she could continue to lay down and sleep. But there were things to be done. The final goodbye was yet to be said.

Krish was up. Deepthi had woken him up. He came into the room and asked Geeta,

"Geeta Ma, can I use the bathroom?"

"Go ahead! I will go after you."

Geeta was glad she could get some more time to herself. Vibha walked into the room and lay beside her. They hugged and continued lying down. Vaishnavi walked in next and lay on Geeta. After a while Krish came out of the bathroom and he lay on the other side next to Geeta. They all lay there hugging each other. Neither wanted to move or go anywhere. Mom in law came up to the room saying,

"Shweta called! You will have to leave in an hour's time. It's a 3-hour drive to the place. It's better to finish before lunch time. If it rains you will get delayed further. "

"Chalo! Let's start getting ready", Geeta told the children. One by one they got up and started getting ready. Geeta dragged herself from the bed and started getting ready to leave. She moved around as if in a dream. She got ready, had her tea and waited for Jiju to pick them up. Dad had finished his tea. He saw Geeta sitting on the sofa. He called out to her and asked,

"When is the wedding?"

"There is no wedding, Dad"

"Oh! I thought you were all going to the wedding, that's why you are dressed up."

"We are just going out for a while."

"The lunch will be good. So, you will be coming after lunch, right? I will miss it"

"Yes Dad. The lunch will be good."

Geeta sighed. Dad was in his own world. It was like dealing with a child.

Jiju drove up to the house, so did Shweta. The girls went with Shweta. Krish, Deepthi and I climbed in with Meghna. We started to the place where the last rites were to be performed. Vidyuth's final journey.

Geeta sat looking outside the window, the last 15 days flashed before her eyes. Vidyuth in the hospital, his final stages when she lost him forever, the cremation. Her chest felt heavy, she was breathing fast and tears rolled down her cheeks. She looked away, out of the window and quietly wiped her tears.

Vidyuth's uncles had collected the ashes and they were on their way as well. Everybody met up at a breakfast place. Geeta saw a few stray dogs walking around. Vidyuth loved dogs. He would have fed them biscuits if he were there. She saw Vibha petting the dogs and feeding them scraps of the breakfast they had. She was a splitting image of Vidyuth and shared the same love and passion for dogs like he did. Geeta smiled as she knew father and daughter would have done this together. She remembered the time when Vibha and Vidyuth had gone to buy dinner. Vibha had come back home excited,

"Mama! You are not going to believe this"

Geeta knew it had to do with dogs or puppies.

"We picked up the food and were waiting at the railway crossing. There were 3 puppies playing in the sand. We gave them 2 chapatis and I pet them. They were so cute Mama! I asked Dada if I could get one home."

"Really !"

"Dada said Mama will throw us out of the house. "

"Yes! He is right. Good you didn't bring one home"

"They were cute but were well fed. I knew they were being looked after so discouraged her from bringing one home", Vidyuth had said.

Vidyuth and Vibha were capable of bringing home all the puppies.

It was time to continue our journey. We finally reached the Sangam. The priest was ready for us. Krish was asked to change into a dhoti, was made to sit on the floor and the priest asked him to recite after him. The urn with ashes was placed in the front while the rituals were being performed. Geeta stood beside Meghna. She couldn't believe that was all that was left of Vidyuth - his ashes. She didn't realise when she had started crying. Meghna put her arms around Geeta and held her. Geeta said a silent prayer for him. The rituals took over an hour. The priest asked Geeta to sit beside him and explained to her the significance of what the children were doing. Geeta was glad she could be a part of it too. Felt like she was helping Vidyuth's soul find peace. Once the rituals were complete, the urn was thrown into the flowing river. Geeta felt like a part of her was flowing away too. Her life, her love, her world was flowing away with the river.

"What do I do without you Vidyuth? How do I go on?" Geeta wanted to scream.

She watched as the children offered the rice to the crows. She stood there for a while until Jiju said they should return. She dragged herself back, thanked the priest and walked towards the car. There was an emptiness she couldn't explain. There was an ache she couldn't explain. She got into the car and they all drove in silence.

Geeta lost track of time. She watched the traffic go by, she watched as the sun went down and the traffic lights were starting to get switched on. Vidyuth loved watching the sunset, she would now watch it alone. She would never go on long drives with him, they would never have family dinners together, they would never be a family again.

They got back home. Geeta had still not spoken much with the mothers. She just didn't know what to say. She knew no words would comfort them. Nothing she said would make things any better. Cause nothing anybody said comforted her.

It had been a long day; they all had dinner and went to bed early. Geeta lay down thinking about the days that had gone by. She was getting tired, she was drained mentally, physically and emotionally.

She didn't know if she would ever be ok, didn't know if she would ever feel better. She pulled the bath robe around her, curled up into a foetal position and closed her eyes.

9

Present Day

It was Vibha's birthday. Vaishnavi was up early. She sneaked into Geeta's room and said,

"Mama, when do we collect the cake?"

They had ordered a unicorn cake. The cook had made lunch and Akanksha had made pasta for the kiddie party. Vidyuth's uncles and cousins would be there. Vibha was excited. Vaishnavi was excited too. They were ready early, had breakfast, wore pretty clothes and helped Mummy clean up the house. Geeta got out all the balloons and the streamers and waited for Vidyuth's cousins to help put them up. Rocky was excited too. He knew something was happening.

Vidyuth's uncles and cousins arrived for lunch. Vibha was excited, she received a lot of gifts. Vibha loved to paint – she received canvas boards, a canvas stand and lots of paints. Vaishnavi also received gifts. When it came to birthdays, the rule was simple. The birthday girl received special gifts and the other received gifts - but both would receive gifts. That way everybody was happy.

After lunch all the youngsters got busy blowing balloons and putting up the streamers. The cake was delivered. The neighbours lend tables and chairs for the kids to sit on. When everything was set, Vibha cut the cake, everybody sang for her.

While the kids were enjoying the cake and snacks, Geeta watched Vibha. She seemed very happy. Her friends were there with her, family was around, she loved the gifts. Everything was perfect. Vidyuth would have liked the way everything had turned out. Geeta missed Vidyuth even more then. She could imagine him interacting with everybody, cracking jokes, engaging the children in games and handing out balloons to them. Whenever they had guests at home, Vidyuth would serve them and Geeta would sit around, relax and chat.

Geeta sighed, as much as she missed Vidyuth she was glad she celebrated Vibha's birthday. After tea, the uncles and cousins left. The kids had started playing and then went to the park to continue playing. Geeta cleared all the tables, put the remaining cake inside. She went upstairs and decided to watch something on tv. She couldn't decide what to watch. She flipped through channels and finally settled on watching an animated movie. Kung Fu panda was one of her favourites. She and Po shared something in common – they both hated stairs. Geeta laughed to herself.

The girls walked in after their games and sat with Geeta to watch Kung Fu Panda. They had a good time. After the movie, Geeta asked Vibha,

"Did you have fun?"

"Yes Mama. It was really nice. Everybody enjoyed it."

"How did you like the cake?"

"The cake was very nice, Mama. Not very sweet. The baker really made it well. The unicorn and the decorations on the cake were very nice too."

"I am glad you liked it. Did you open all your gifts?"

"No, we will do it now."

Geeta got up and went into her room. She decided to rest a while before dinner.

Dad was calling out to her, so Geeta walked down the stairs to him,

"It was so noisy", he complained, "have all the people gone? They must have enjoyed it. So how was the wedding?"

Dad had no recollection of having had the cake, meeting the people. He didn't remember that he had wished Vibha for her birthday. But Geeta knew there was no point reminding him. It was a matter of time and he would forget it again. So, she said,

"Everything went off well, Dad."

"Good. It was nicely arranged. Small and decent crowd." Saying this he walked back into his room.

Geeta went back upstairs. She heard her phone ring. It was Ranjini, her colleague from way back when she worked. "How are you? It was Vibha's birthday, wasn't it? "

"Yes, it was. Had some kids come over and family was there too. The girls had fun."

"Good, you celebrated her birthday. She must have been very happy. How are you coping?"

"I am fine."

"Look Geeta! You know you can call me anytime. Don't keep your feelings bottled in. It just doesn't help. I know it's tough on you and there is not much I can do to help. But I am there for you, anytime you want to speak call me."

"Yes, I will."

"Ok. Take care. Will call you again in a few days."

Geeta slumped back on the pillows. She knew what her friend had said was right. But Geeta was a very private person. She never shared her life with people. And now it was difficult to change. She felt a surge of emotions and the urge to emote. She knew the best way to do that was to write. She looked for a book and found Vidyuth's notebook. She borrowed a pen from the girls and penned her thoughts.

"I live every moment in conflicting thoughts

While I enjoy the beautiful morning, I also feel loneliness

While I feel the love of my children, I also feel the loss

While I look towards building a future, I think of the future that will never be

While I see the happiness around me, I feel the pain in me

While I am told time heals, I wonder what scars it will leave

While I enjoy the view of the open fields, I can't see beyond today

While I believe I am strong I can feel the cracks in my being

While I know I will be fine I also know I will never be me again."

Geeta read what she had written. Satisfied with how it had turned out she excused herself from dinner, kissed the girls goodnight and went to sleep. She knew she had taken the first step towards being completely independent. And this was the first among the many steps she would take in the days to come.

It had been 3 months since Vidyuth had passed. Geeta had been busy handling legal documents, insurance and of course people visiting her to extend their condolences. Life was limping back to normalcy. The girls were busy with school, music classes and sports. Geeta had now started walking the dogs, she needed the distraction. She needed something to get her out of bed, something for her to look forward to. She enjoyed the early morning walks. The dogs loved it too – sniffing the lamp posts and trees, chasing birds, staring down at other dogs, running to people to be pet. She walked the dogs in the evening too. Vibha accompanied her in the morning. She enjoyed the walks just as much as the dogs did.

Geeta enjoyed the morning breeze, the green grass moist with dew, and seeing other dogs going for walks. It filled her with energy. She also re-joined yoga sessions that she had taken a break from. A rather long break she felt. She had formed a routine and tried to stick to it as far as possible. She began clearing up the rooms, rearranging furniture and decluttering. She decided to spend time gardening. Touching the soil and planting saplings gave her a sense of achievement. It calmed her down.

She still had trouble sleeping. She would tire herself out so she could sleep at night. But no matter how hard she tried she would wake up at the slightest noise and would remain awake tossing and turning until daybreak. She met her neighbours, spent time with them, and went out shopping with them. She would laugh and gossip yet something seemed missing. There were days she felt so sleep deprived that she would sleep all morning, afternoon and night waking up only for meals.

Every time she spent on groceries and made purchases; she was reminded of the fact that she was eating away into the savings. She knew she had to get back onto the job circuit. But she felt so ill prepared, so under qualified, her confidence was shaken. It had been a while since she had worked. She knew she could face any challenge thrown at her, but for some reason the very thought of going back to work gave her cold feet. The world had changed so much since she last worked at an office. Going back to that space, facing peers younger to her, probably more experienced than she was made her palms sweat. She knew she had to get over that feeling, she just didn't know how.

Neighbours and friends were more than willing to help. They gave her references, volunteered to forward her resume to people they knew. Geeta was grateful. But confidence was still low.

Geeta asked herself- what is the worst that could happen? She won't be chosen. At least she would have tried and every interview would be an experience. But nothing seemed to help. "I will get over this'', she would tell herself.

One morning Geeta received a call from an old friend. Seeing the name flash on the phone brought a smile to her face. It had been a long time since they had connected. Geeta answered the call.

"How are you, Geeta? asked the voice at the other end. It had been so long since Geeta had heard that voice. She had been so busy with her family life that she had not been in touch with most of her friends.

"I am doing fine, Sanjay. How have you been?"

"I am glad you are well. I wasn't sure when I could call."

"I understand. I received your texts. Just been tied up with paperwork. "

"It's good to hear your voice again after all these years."

"It has been a while hasn't it!"

And just like that it was like old times, friends chatting up, catching up on all the missing time. Geeta was transported to a time when life was a lot less complicated.

They had a long chat. Geeta felt good. She felt young again. There was something about old friends. It was so easy speaking to an old friend, there were no expectations and no pretences. With renewed energy, Geeta pulled up her resume, went to job sites and decided to apply for roles that suited her best.

It was a tedious process, most times Geeta felt that she was under qualified for the roles. It seemed quite overwhelming. The enthusiasm seemed to be dying down slowly. She decided to give the job hunt a break and diverted her mind to reading. She borrowed some books from Meghna and immersed herself in adventures of Jack Ryan, the Warwick chronicles and whatever would transport her away from the present.

Geeta had been struggling with some property related issues that she didn't seem to get her head around. She needed to speak to somebody who could give her an unbiased opinion. She called Sanjay. He was very helpful. He had people who knew that could help. Geeta was relieved.

"How are you coping?", Sanjay asked.

"I am living one day at a time."

"Hmmm! I know it's tough but you do realise you have to go on. For the girls, for mom and dad and more importantly for yourself."

"I know Sanjay. I am trying to find a job. It is just so difficult. Any other time, it wouldn't have mattered what I did or how soon I found work. Now it's like a pressure situation and I am not able to think clearly."

"Take your time. You are a confident person, capable of handling pressure situations. You have done so, so many times in your life. For all that you have been through, you are still standing. That's commendable. You need to start believing in yourself. I know there is no magic wand which you can wave and make things possible. But don't let small setbacks disappoint you."

"It's easier said than done."

"I know. I am sorry. I know I am not helping."

"Don't feel sorry. I am just all over the place at the moment. I have started pushing away people who care for me."

"Ok. Let's talk about something else. Have you been doing any writing? "

"Writing! Not really. Have penned down some thoughts. Nothing serious."

"Why don't you start writing? You do have a flair for writing. I remember some of the stuff you shared a long time back."

"I don't know, Sanjay. I don't even know if any of those creative juices will flow."

"Give it a try. Write about something you are passionate about or maybe a story. Something to take your mind off all that is happening around you. I believe it will help."

"Maybe. I haven't thought about it though. Let's see."

"Well! you know whom to call to bounce back ideas with. Take care!"

Geeta smiled. It was always very easy talking to Sanjay. Writing! thought Geeta. What could she write about? She remembered the stories she would tell the girls when they were younger. But that didn't interest her. She sat thinking and looking out of the window. She had a dejavu moment. She knew what she would write about! She pulled out the laptop, opened a blank word document and started writing

---

Tripthi looked outside the window. She enjoyed the view from her room - open fields, the greenery, watching the cows and goats graze, the cow herds accompanied by their dogs keeping the herd in check, watching the flights taking off...................